Malik and the Magic Bowtie

WRITTEN BY
RAY YOUNG JR.

ILLUSTRATED BY
TYRUS GOSHAY

Malik and The magic Bowtie

Tgosketch
Illustration
www.tgosketch.com

Acknowledgment

I would like to first thank God for allowing me to write this book. Thank you to my lovely wife, who is supportive and always encouraging me when it comes to my vision. Thank you to my wonderful son that is such a joy and who gave me the inspiration to write this book. Thank you to my mom and dad, who always give me encouraging words and wisdom. Thank you to my brothers and my sister for supporting your big brother. Thank you to my extended family for your support as well. Lastly, I want to thank Mr. John Oliver for his contribution to the book.

It was the Day Before the election, and Malik was writing his speech. He was in a race for **Class President!**

He stayed up all weekend preparing. Malik's dad walked into his son's room and noticed all the crumpled pieces of paper on the floor.

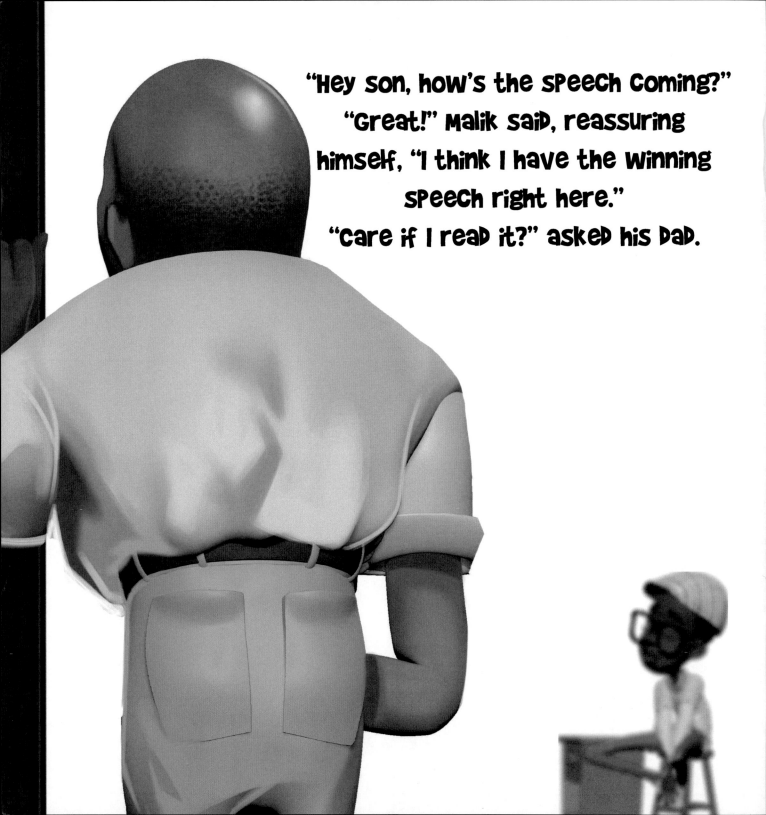

Malik shook his head yes and handed over the paper.

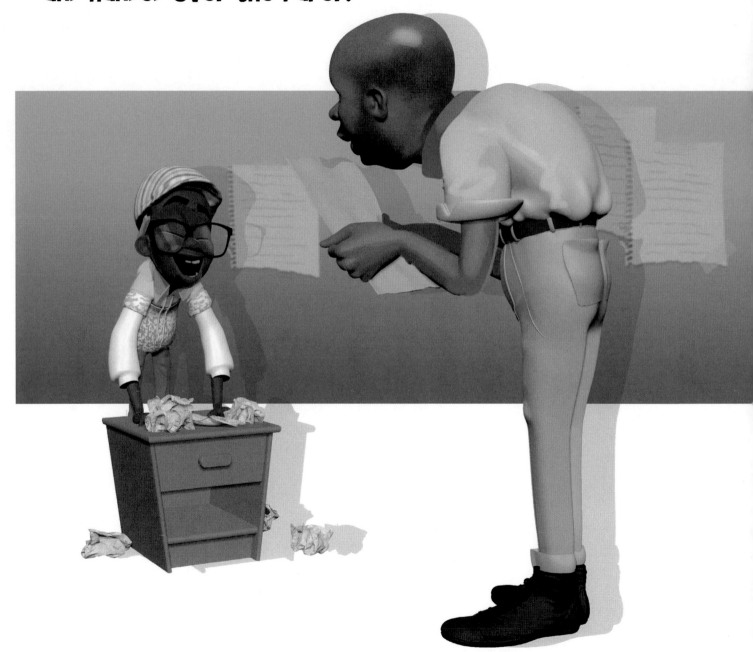

"Wait, wait, wait, you ran for Class President?"

"I sure did," Malik's dad said proudly, "I won too."

Malik started to feel discouraged, "I don't know what I'm doing. I'll never win class president. There's not one kid in the whole class who looks like me, and I don't have very many friends. I've been trying to secure votes. I've done everything I could and they still don't like me."

"I understand son, I looked different from my classmates too, and I also didn't have many friends." His dad said with his hand on Malik's shoulder, "Wait here. I have something for you." Malik's dad went into his room and returned with a small red box.

"What's this?" Malik asked as he reached for the box and uncovered a bow tie.

"This Bow tie was mine, and it was my father's and Before that his father's. This Bow tie has Been in the family for generations, and it is going to help you win that title."

Malik looked at the tie, Confused, "Sure, it's a great tie, But nobody wears ties like this anymore, Dad. People are going to laugh at me."

"Magic? What do you mean it's magic?"

"You'll see!" his Dad said as he walked away.

Malik was feeling nervous about his big speech. He also knew the importance of a good night's sleep. He looked over his speech one more time and went to bed.

The next morning, while Malik got ready for school, he put on his regular tie. He stared in his closet at his Dad's magical Bow tie and decided to put it in his Book Bag, just in case.

"Hey, Malik!" Stanley, the class bully, yelled across the cafeteria. "Ready for today's election? I hope you brought a box of tissues for your tears after you lose!" Malik's classmates laughed, and he ran to the bathroom.

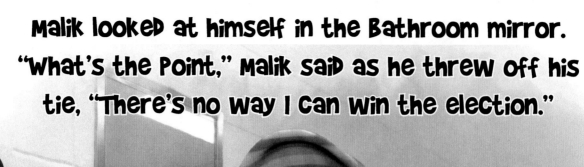

Malik looked at himself in the Bathroom mirror. "What's the Point," Malik said as he threw off his tie, "There's no way I can win the election."

Just then, Malik remembered his Dad's words.

"They might laugh, But you shouldn't care what they think. Besides, this tie is magic!"

That Morning, Malik Decided to wear his father's bow tie, and once it was on, he knew he looked sharp. As he walked to class prepared to deliver his speech, he felt like a winner and smiled confidently.

When his teacher called him up to present his speech, he put his paper down and spoke from his heart.

"As your Class President, I Promise to Do more than just Bring you Pizza Parties every month, and Create a new recess schedule.
I Promise to stand up for the students who are Bullied. I Promise to listen to your ProBlems, and I Promise to Be true to myself. I hope it encourages you to Be true to yourselves too."

Malik won the election that Day, as well as the respect from his classmates.

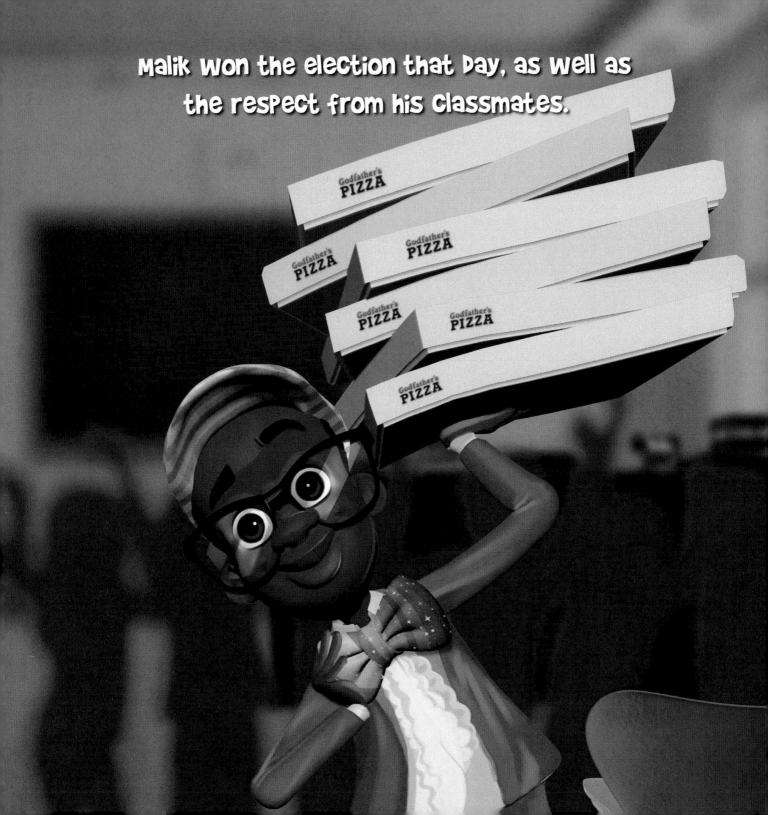

As he walked in the house with his bowtie still tied, he smiled at his dad and said,

"You're right, this tie is magic!"

About the Author:

Ray Young, Jr. is a native of Waco, Texas, and has overcome many obstacles in life. Malik and the Magic Bowtie is his first book. Mr. Young has a Bachelor's degree, two Master's Degrees and plans to continue his education in a doctorate program. Mr. Young is a certified Life Coach and motivational speaker. He is the CEO and Founder of a nonprofit called Young's Vision Achievement Consulting as well as the Owner and Founder of the MYGO brand, which means "My Greatness Overcomes." Mr. Young has many awards and achievements, including the National Service Award through AmeriCorps.

Malik and the Magic Bowtie

Email: ray.young81@gmail.com

malik_magicbowtie

www.yvaconsulting.com
www.mygo-brand.com

About The Illustrator:

Tyrus Goshay is an award-winning digital illustrator and 3D artist with over 18 years of experience. He serves as a college professor, teaching both game design and illustration in his off time. Tyrus has a bachelor's in Computer Animation and Multimedia and a master's degree in Teaching With Technology (MALT). He has contributed to several award-winning projects in the world of toy design and has been recognized for his achievements in academia as well. He also has tutorials in illustration and digital sculpting available on the web. I want to send a special shout out to my Art Assistant Elizabeth Teran. Thank you for your "Weekend Warrior" support. Connect With Tgosketch Illustration at:

www.Facebook.com/tgosketch

Email:tgosketch@gmail.com

Instagram:@tgosketch

Made in the USA
Las Vegas, NV
21 February 2024